Disney PRINCESS

palace pets

Pumpkin

Cinderella's Dancing Pup

For Ava Hunter —T.R.

Disney PRINCESS

palace pets

Pumpkin

Cinderella's Dancing Pup

By Tennant Redbank

Illustrated by Francesco Legramandi
and Gabriella Matta

Random House 🏠 New York

Pumpkin growled. Something was out of place in Cinderella's room. There, on the bed! A flat, square pink thing stuck out from under Cinderella's pillow. It didn't belong!

Cinderella kept her room spotless. For years, she had cleaned for her stepmother and stepsisters. Now she lived in a castle with the Prince and had lots of help, but she was still very tidy. She dusted and swept. She always made her bed. She put away every gown and crown.

Pumpkin looked at Cinderella. She was brushing her hair and singing. She wasn't going to take care of the thing under her pillow. Well, Pumpkin would! The Prince had given Pumpkin to Cinderella as a present, and Pumpkin had looked out for her ever since. They were best friends!

Pumpkin stalked the object, moving slowly across the floor. Her paws didn't make a sound. She leaped onto the bed. She crawled on her belly across the blanket toward the pillow.

She lowered her ears. She raised her tail. Then . . .

Pumpkin gave a warning bark and pounced! She snatched the square thing between her teeth. Growling, she shook it back and forth.

"Pumpkin! What's wrong?" Cinderella

asked as she rushed to the bed.

Pumpkin raised her eyes to Cinderella.
She tried to look fierce, but her tail gave
her away. It was wagging.

Cinderella noticed the square thing
in Pumpkin's mouth. "What's that?" she
asked.

Pumpkin dropped the thing on
Cinderella's pillow. It didn't move. In fact,
it didn't seem very dangerous anymore.

"It's an envelope!" Cinderella said.

An envelope? Hmm, Cinderella was
right. How could Pumpkin have known

that from across the room? Embarrassed, she backed away.

Cinderella read the envelope. "It says 'To Cinderella and Pumpkin'!"

She knelt and Pumpkin put her paws on Cinderella's knees. How exciting! It was a surprise, and Pumpkin had found it!

Cinderella neatly opened the envelope. She pulled out a fancy piece of paper.

"It's an invitation to a ball! Tomorrow at eight o'clock in the garden. 'Don't be late!' it says." Cinderella laughed. "Oh,

Pumpkin! Ever since I was late to my first ball, people always think I'll be late."

Pumpkin sniffed the invitation. She felt bad about the teeth marks on it. But a ball! Pumpkin loved balls! Balls meant dancing. And dancing was Pumpkin's

absolute favorite thing in the world!

"I haven't told you the best part, Pumpkin," Cinderella said. She rubbed the fur between Pumpkin's ears. "It's not just any ball. It's a masquerade ball. That means we'll dress up in costumes!"

Dancing *and* costumes? Pumpkin barked. She couldn't imagine anything more exciting!

Pumpkin woke up with the sun. The ball—it was today! She jumped onto the bed and stood on Cinderella's back. The princess barely moved. Pumpkin licked her face.

Cinderella put an arm over her eyes.

"Too early!" she groaned. "First the Prince woke me up when he went out riding. Now you! Sleep. Need more sleeee . . ."

Cinderella rolled onto her side and went silent.

Pumpkin tilted her head. Why wasn't Cinderella more excited? It was okay, though. Pumpkin was excited enough for both of them!

Pumpkin bounced off the bed. She spun in circles on the floor. Today! Today! The ball was today! Then she spun the other way . . . just because she could.

Much about the ball was still a mystery. Who had sent the invitation? Was it Gus and Jaq, her mouse friends? Was it Bibbidy the pony? Was it Bruno the dog? The only one Pumpkin could rule out was Cinderella, because the invitation was for her, too!

Pumpkin had another question. What costume should she wear?

She could be a fairy. Or a pirate. Or a spider! A spy! An angel! There were so many choices! She had even thought of dressing up like a cat. But no . . . that was silly.

Pumpkin scratched her ear with her back paw. Choosing a costume was hard! She could worry about that later. Right now, she would practice dancing. After all, that was the most important part of a ball!

Pumpkin dashed out of Cinderella's bedroom. She pranced down the white marble stairs. Outside, dew shone on the grass and the leaves of the trees. The marble terrace, too, was covered in dew.

The sun was out, and a slight breeze was blowing. Perfect weather for dancing! Pumpkin stood in the middle of the terrace. She bowed to an imaginary partner. Then she started to twirl. She twirled to her left. She twirled to her right. The trees around her blurred. She closed her eyes. She twirled and twirled and twirled and—

"Pumpkin! Watch out!"

It was Bibbidy. What was she shouting about? Pumpkin's eyes sprang open.

Oh! She was inches away from falling

over the edge of the terrace!

She tried to stop, but her paws slipped on the dew. Pumpkin slid toward the edge of the terrace. . . .

Luckily, a bush stopped her.

Unfortunately, it was a rosebush . . . with thorns! Ouch!

Bibbidy cantered over and looked down at Pumpkin. "Are you okay?" she asked.

Pumpkin stared back at her. Why was Bibbidy upside down? Then she realized Bibbidy wasn't upside down. *She* was!

"I'm okay!" Pumpkin answered. She rolled out of the bush. She got to her paws.

Ow, ouch, ow, ow, owie!

She raised one paw. *Oh, drat!* Something long and sharp was stuck in it. It was a thorn. A big one!

"Nope! Not okay," Pumpkin corrected herself.

"That looks like it hurts," Bibbidy said. "I'll get Cinderella!"

"Oh, Pumpkin," Cinderella said. She held Pumpkin's paw in her hands and shook her head. Behind her, Bibbidy shook her head, too. "How do you get into such messes?"

Messes? What was Cinderella talking about? Pumpkin never got into messes! Well . . . there was that time she fell into the pigpen. And when she got stung by a bumblebee. And the time—

Never mind! Why think about stuff like that?

"This might hurt a little," Cinderella warned. She took the thorn between her fingers.

Pumpkin gritted her teeth.

Cinderella gently pulled the thorn out. Pumpkin was brave. And it hardly hurt at all!

"There," Cinderella said. "Now I'll fix it up."

Cinderella cleaned Pumpkin's paw. Then she wrapped a soft white bandage around it. She tied the bandage snug with a knot.

"How's that?" Cinderella asked. "Go on! Give it a try!"

Bibbidy and Cinderella watched as Pumpkin carefully stood up. So far, so good! She took a step. It hurt a little.

Pumpkin tried to twirl—

Ow, ouch, ow, ow, owie!

Nope, dancing was no good. She'd have to settle for walking . . . with a limp. But how could she go to the ball if she couldn't dance? What fun would that be?

"Try to stay off it." Cinderella gave Pumpkin's hurt paw a kiss, then went back inside.

Stay off her paw? Pumpkin rolled onto

her back and looked at the sky. The day

stretched long before her. A day without

dancing would be boring!

"I bet Cinderella is going to work on

her costume again," Bibbidy said.

Pumpkin sighed. "I guess," she said.

"I should work on my costume, too,"

said Bibbidy.

"I guess," Pumpkin said again.

"*You* should work on *your* costume,"

Bibbidy told her friend.

"I guess— Hey!" Pumpkin rolled over.

Her tail began to wag. "That's right!

I have to make my costume! I'm going to be a fairy-pirate-spider-spy-angel! It'll be perfect!"

Bibbidy looked doubtful. "That sounds complicated. But I know who can help us. The mice! They've been helping Cinderella. She just made a beautiful mask with them."

Yes! Bibbidy was right. The mice were good at making costumes and dresses.

Pumpkin leaped to her feet.

OUCH!

She lifted her hurt paw. She had to

remember not to use it for a while.

Pumpkin limped behind Bibbidy into the castle. They went to the mouse work space. The mice were already making their costumes for the ball.

Pumpkin explained her idea to Jaq.

"You're going to be a fairy-pirate-spider-spy-angel?" he repeated. He pulled on his whiskers. "Hmm . . . start with the mask. *Zup, zup!*"

He brought out two plain white masks. One was for Pumpkin. The other was for her friend Bibbidy.

Gus pointed to some pots of colorful paint. "Got lots of paint," he said. "And feathers. And glitter. And buttons. And beads . . ."

So many colors! Pumpkin dove right in. She was feeling red today. And maybe a little yellow.

Pumpkin used her paws to spread the

paint on the white mask. The red and yellow paint smeared together and made orange. But that was okay. Pumpkin liked orange, too!

The mask still needed something. Feathers! She found some colorful feathers. They would look good with the orange. She backed up for a better view . . . and knocked over a pot of glue.

Oh, well! She needed glue for the feathers anyway. With the mice's help, she stuck them on the mask. It wasn't quite what she had pictured, but—

"I'm done!" Bibbidy said. "Want to see?" In front of the pony was a gorgeous blue mask. There was a large pink bow on either side.

"Oh, Bibbidy," Pumpkin said. "It's beautiful!"

She looked at her mask again. The orange paint was a little spotty. Red and orange feathers stuck out from both sides. She went to move one of the feathers, but something was wrong with her paws—they were orange! And they were stuck together!

Bibbidy whinnied with laughter. "Pumpkin, how do you get into such messes?" she said. She sounded just like Cinderella.

Pumpkin laughed. "I don't mean to!" she said. Then she rolled around the workshop floor, trying to pull her paws apart.

That glue was strong!

There mice pulled on one paw. Three more mice pulled on the other. Finally, Pumpkin's paws popped apart. The mice wiped them clean.

Pumpkin's mask was all done, and she was proud of it. She didn't want to take it off. She left it on top of her head.

Now she had to figure out the rest of her costume.

She turned to Jaq. "Where do you keep the wings?" she asked.

Jaq frowned. "Wings?" he said.

"The fairy wings. For my costume," Pumpkin said.

"Don't think we have—"

"And I need a pirate hat. A spy cloak. Eight black spider legs. And a golden halo," Pumpkin went on. "Then I'll be ready!"

Jaq thought for a second. He scampered to a box on the worktable, which was full of bows and ribbons and lace. He rummaged through it.

"Aha!" he said, pulling out a long strip of black cloth. "Look! A spy cloak. *Zup, zup!* But I don't have the other things. The wings and legs and hat and halo. Have to find them yourself."

"Thanks, Jaq!" Pumpkin said, bouncing on her paws.

Ouch!

She kept forgetting about her hurt paw.

All morning, Pumpkin searched for bits of her costume. But it wasn't easy.

She found a pirate hat in the Prince's wardrobe. He wouldn't mind if she borrowed it! Why did the Prince have a pirate hat anyway?

After that, her luck ran out. She tried to make fairy wings out of silk kites, but they were a flop. She painted eight sticks black, but they didn't look like spider legs. They just looked like eight black sticks.

And the halo? Pumpkin was stumped.

Pumpkin and Bibbidy sat together in front of Pumpkin's costume. A black spy cloak and a pirate hat. Oh, and the mask. At least Pumpkin had her mask.

Well, she wouldn't be a fairy-pirate-spider-spy-angel this time. She'd just be a puppy-spy-pirate.

Then her tummy rumbled. Bibbidy gave her a look.

"Pumpkin, did you have breakfast today?"

Pumpkin shook her head. She'd been too excited to eat!

"Did you have lunch?" Bibbidy asked.

"Nope," Pumpkin said. She'd been too busy looking for her costume!

"You have to eat something," Bibbidy said.

Yes! Bibbidy was right. Pumpkin was very hungry.

The kitchen was always crazy before a ball. But Pumpkin knew a secret spot for getting food. The springhouse! The gardener stored fresh fruits and vegetables there. Tomatoes, red and ripe. Potatoes with dirt still on them. Grapes just off the vine. Carrots pulled right out of the ground. And a big bag of puppy treats. He was Pumpkin's friend.

Pumpkin's paw twinged with pain when she stood up. She was still learning to take it easy. She might not be able to dance at the ball, but she'd be there to have fun with her friends!

"I'm going to get some lunch," Pumpkin said. "I mean, breakfast. Or maybe dinner— Oh, I don't know!"

"Better hurry!" Bibbidy told her. "The ball is at eight o'clock. You still need to put on your costume."

"I won't be late!" Pumpkin said.

The springhouse was tucked away at the back of the garden. Pine trees shaded it. A little creek trickled past. Moss covered the roof.

Pumpkin nudged the wooden door open with her nose. Cool air greeted her. So did the smell of dirt. And the smell of puppy treats!

Pumpkin looked around. Where

were they? She didn't see a single treat anywhere.

She peeked into a bag. Potatoes.

She checked another bag. Nope. Tomatoes.

In one corner was a bag of carrots, peppers, and squash. There were even a few round orange pumpkins!

Pumpkin shut her eyes and sniffed the air. There! She could smell the treats. She followed her nose. Silly gardener! He had stuck the puppy treats all the way in

the back, behind the squash.

Pumpkin pulled the sack open with her teeth and dug in. *Yum, yum, yummy, yum, yum.* She loved treats! She loved the crunch of them. She loved the taste of—

BANG!

Pumpkin jumped. What was that? She spun around.

Oh. Phew. It was just the door to the springhouse. The wind must have blown it shut.

Pumpkin ate two more treats. Then she gnawed on a carrot. Soon her belly felt full. Good. She needed to get ready for the ball!

Pumpkin walked to the springhouse

door and pushed it with her nose.

Nothing happened.

She pushed it harder.

Still nothing.

She stood on her back paws and pushed with her front paw, the one that wasn't hurt. Hard. Harder. *Arrrrgh!*

Nope. The door didn't move.

Pumpkin growled at the door.

The door didn't care.

She scratched at the floor at the bottom of the door. It was packed hard. With only one good paw, it would take her all night

to dig out. And then what? She would miss the ball!

Aaaaaaooooooh! Pumpkin howled. She was so loud, she scared herself. Someone had to hear her!

But no one came.

Pumpkin was trapped! She might be stuck here forever! Or at least until the gardener showed up.

Cinderella and Bibbidy were right. How did she get into such messes?

Pumpkin lay down on the floor. She put her head on her paws. Out of the corner of her eye, she saw something twinkle.

Pumpkin raised her head. What was that?

There! There it was again. Light sparkled behind the grapes. Maybe it was a lightning bug!

Pumpkin got up to check it out. *Oh!* There was a crack in the springhouse wall! It wasn't very big, but neither was Pumpkin. Maybe this was her way out!

Pumpkin squeezed past a crate of grapes. The vines got tangled in her fur. She pushed forward until she snapped loose from the twisty vines.

She crawled along the wall to the crack. She could see outside! She wiggled her head through the crack. She wiggled her paws through. She wiggled her back through. And her tail wiggled itself through.

She was free!

From the castle tower, the clock began to chime. It was eight o'clock! She was going to be late for the ball!

Pumpkin raced through the trees. She dashed across the grass. She dodged rocks and roots. Up ahead, she saw lights. It was the garden!

Round orange paper lanterns lined the pathway. Blue-and-white banners hung from the trees. Silk flags waved in the breeze. Pumpkin was almost there!

She was running so fast, her mask

slipped. It fell over her eyes. All the feathers on her mask fell off when she shook it straight. But, *oh!* An unlit lantern had fallen to the ground in her path. She couldn't swerve out of the way in time! Pumpkin crashed inside the lantern headfirst. She tried to shake it off, but it was stuck around her legs and belly. She poked her paws out the top and got back up. She started running again.

"Cinderella! Bibbidy! Jaq! Wait for me!" she cried. "I'm coming!"

Pumpkin skidded into the garden.

She was already panting hard, and the sight of the ball took away the rest of her breath. The lanterns. The banners. And the costumes! It was all so beautiful!

Cinderella stood in the middle of the garden. She wore a shimmery blue-and-white gown. There were sparkly wings on her back. She was a fairy!

Next to her, the Prince was dressed as a pirate. He wore a puffy white shirt and an eye patch. But no hat. *Hmm.*

The mice wore long ears and had cottonballs tied over their tails. They were little bunnies! Bruno was covered in white powder and black ink spots. He wasn't a hound dog anymore. He was a Dalmatian.

Best of all was Bibbidy. She had added a golden horn to her mask. Bibbidy was a pretty little unicorn!

Their costumes were so nice. If only

Pumpkin had one, too!

She sighed. Well, at least she had her mask.

Bibbidy trotted over. "You made it!" she said. "Isn't the ball wonderful? Guess who did all this—the Prince!"

"The Prince? I never thought of him!" Pumpkin said. "Oh, Bibbidy! You won't believe what happened. I got trapped in the springhouse! I just got out! I didn't have time to put on my costume!"

"What do you mean?" Bibbidy said. "Your costume is perfect. I like it even better than the puppy-spy-pirate idea."

Pumpkin tilted her head. What was Bibbidy talking about?

"Go take a look in the fountain," Bibbidy said.

Pumpkin went to the fountain. Torches lit the water. She found her reflection. *Oh! Look at that!* An orange mask. An orange lantern around her middle.

And a curly grapevine on her head.

Pumpkin was . . . a pumpkin!

"There you are, my little pumpkin!"
Cinderella said. "What a perfect costume!"
She swept Pumpkin into her arms. "I
didn't think you would make it, but then
I saw you dash into the garden. I'm so
happy your paw feels better!"

Better? Her paw? What—?

Wait a second. . . . Cinderella was
right! Pumpkin had run here from the
springhouse. She had dashed through the
grass. She had raced through the trees.

And her paw hadn't hurt once. It was all better!

Now the ball would be just wonderful!

A band began to play a lively waltz. Pumpkin wiggled out of Cinderella's arms. As soon as her paws hit the ground, she started dancing. And she didn't stop all night. Not when the clock struck nine. Or ten. Or eleven.

Not even when the clock struck midnight.

Cinderella

Bibbidy

Snow White

Berry

Aurora

Dreamy

to tell—collect them all!

Belle

Teacup

Tiana

Lily

Ariel

Seashell